The Iliad

Retold from the Homer original
by Kathleen Olmstead

Illustrated by Eric Freeberg

STERLING CHILDREN'S BOOKS
New York

STERLING CHILDREN'S BOOKS
New York

An Imprint of Sterling Publishing Co., Inc.
1166 Avenue of the Americas
New York, NY 10036

ISBN 978-1-4549-0612-4

Library of Congress Cataloging-in-Publication Data
Olmstead, Kathleen.
  The Iliad / retold by Kathleen Olmstead ; illustrations by Eric Freeberg.
    pages cm. -- (Classic starts)
  ISBN 978-1-4549-0612-4
  1. Achilles (Greek mythology)--Juvenile literature. 2. Trojan War--Juvenile
literature. I. Freeberg, Eric, illustrator. II. Homer. Iliad. III. Title.
  BL820.A22O46 2014
  808.8'0351--dc23

                                                              2013026604

Distributed in Canada by Sterling Publishing Co., Inc.
c/o Canadian Manda Group, 664 Annette Street
Toronto, Ontario, Canada M6S 2C8
Distributed in the United Kingdom by GMC Distribution Services
Castle Place, 166 High Street, Lewes, East Sussex, England BN7 1XU
Distributed in Australia by NewSouth Books
45 Beach Street, Coogee, NSW 2034, Australia

For information about custom editions, special sales, and premium and
corporate purchases, please contact Sterling Special Sales at
800-805-5489 or specialsales@sterlingpublishing.com.

Manufactured in China

Lot #:
8 10 9
11/19

www.sterlingpublishing.com

CONTENTS

ॐ

Prologue

⌒

The immortal gods and goddesses of Mount Olympus ruled over the lives of mortal humans on earth. Zeus, the god of thunder, was the leader of the gods. His brothers Poseidon, god of the sea, and Hades, god of the underworld, had the power to shake the ocean and the earth. But they were not as mighty as Zeus. Hera, Zeus's wife; Athena, goddess of war; and Aphrodite, goddess of love, could change the weather from sunny to stormy. But they were not as mighty as Zeus. Ares, the god of war, and Apollo, the sun

god and master archer, could change the outcome of a battle. But they were not as mighty as
Zeus. The king of gods could see all. He held the
fate of the world in his hands.

Now, dear reader, you will hear the tale of
Achilles and his rage. Achilles was not a god like
Zeus. But he was a mighty and powerful man. He
was a swift runner and a brave warrior. He was
a hero of the Trojan War, which is the war this
story is about. Achilles was part of the Achaean
army, from Greece. The Achaean army battled
the Trojan army near their home city of Troy.

Achilles held much rage in his heart. That
rage caused many deaths among both Achaeans
and Trojans. But this story does not start with
Achilles. It starts many years earlier with a fight
among three goddesses.

The gods were hosting a banquet at their
home on Mount Olympus. They feasted and
drank. They sang and told stories.

During the meal, Eris, goddess of trouble, left an apple on the table. She had placed a sign next to the apple. This sign said, "For the fairest." Hera, Athena, and Aphrodite all tried to take the apple. Each goddess claimed to be the fairest. They fought over this apple. They asked Zeus to decide who should have the apple, but he refused. He sent the goddesses to visit Paris, prince of the city of Troy. Paris would judge who was the fairest.

Each goddess offered Paris something so that he would call her the fairest. Hera offered him political power. Athena offered him wisdom and strength in battle. Aphrodite offered him the love of the most beautiful woman in the world. Paris chose Aphrodite as the fairest.

Aphrodite sent Paris to the city of Sparta, where Helen lived. Helen was the most beautiful woman in the world. Aphrodite made this woman fall in love with Paris. But Helen was

3

already married to a man named Menelaus. Under Aphrodite's spell, Helen left her husband and went back to Troy with Paris.

Hera and Athena never forgave Paris, or the city of Troy, for not choosing either of them as the fairest. From that moment onward, the two goddesses had great hatred for Troy.

Menelaus felt great hatred for the man who stole his wife. Menelaus's brother, King Agamemnon, declared war on the people of Troy. He wanted revenge—to honor his brother and punish the Trojans. Agamemnon's bravest generals—Menelaus, Nestor, Odysseus, Diomedes, Ajax, and Achilles—joined him in the war. They agreed to follow the king in his quest to destroy Troy and bring Helen home. Each general brought his own ships with troops of soldiers and chariots to drive into battle. Achilles was joined by his closest friend, Patroclus. This mighty group was known as the Achaean army.

The Achaeans fought against the Trojans for nine years. With each battle they moved closer to the city of Troy. But the men were tired after so many years of fighting. They wanted to go home.

King Priam of Troy guarded his city while his oldest son, Hector, led his army. Paris, Priam's younger son, and Aeneas, Aphrodite's son, fought alongside Hector. The Trojan army was strong. That army—led by Pisander, Dolon, Sarpedon, and Teucer—was mighty and brave. The walls of the city were secure. No other army had broken through the gates. The Trojans feared only Achilles, the greatest Achaean fighter.

Achilles was a great warrior and a man of legend. He was the son of a sea goddess named Thetis and a mortal man named Peleus. He was favored by the gods. He was both loved and feared by men—and for good reason. It was Achilles who set this story in motion. His rage was great enough to affect the fates of gods and men.

AENEAS

PARIS

CHRYSES

HECUBA

HECTOR

PRIAM

HELEN

ACHILLES

AGAMEMNON

MENELAUS   ODYSSEUS

AJAX   PATROCLUS   NESTOR   DIOMEDES

CHAPTER 1

Achilles

When our story begins, the Trojan War had been going on for almost ten years. Many battles had been fought, and many men had died. Soldiers and generals from both sides were exhausted. The Achaean men wanted to go home, but they were loyal to King Agamemnon. If he said they should continue fighting, that was what they would do.

Agamemnon and his men had captured many Trojans after an important battle. These people were soldiers and women from a nearby town. The Achaeans planned to sell these Trojans as slaves. One of the prisoners was the daughter of Apollo's priest, Chryses. Chryses begged the Achaeans to free his daughter. He promised them riches in return.

"I will give you more riches than you would make by selling my daughter as a slave," he said.

The Achaean soldiers thought this was a good deal. King Agamemnon did not. He would not give Chryses's daughter back no matter how big the fortune was. In fact, he decided to keep the young woman as his slave rather than sell her.

"Do you think you can control the will of a king? I will not be swayed by your promise of money," Agamemnon told Chryses. "No one, especially a Trojan priest, tells me what I should or should not do!" He laughed at the priest and waved his arm in the air. "Leave now, old man," Agamemnon shouted. "If I see you again, it will mean the end for you *and* your daughter!"

The priest Chryses was terrified. He returned to his ship and set sail for home. The priest prayed to the god Apollo. "Hear me, Apollo! God of the silver bow! You know that I have prayed to you for years. I have built you temples and offered sacrifices to you. Please listen to my prayer now. Claim revenge upon the Achaeans for what they have done to my daughter and me. Send your arrows in place of my tears!"

Apollo heard the old priest's prayer. He protected those who honored him with temples and songs. Apollo strode down from Mount Olympus with his bow and arrows slung over his shoulders. The arrows clanged as the god shook with rage. Apollo dropped to a knee and let an arrow fly near the Achaean ships. A terrifying clash rang out from the great silver bow. Then he shot arrow after arrow at the Achaean ships.

The men were not expecting this attack. They were unprepared for such force. Apollo's arrows rained over their camps night and day with no end in sight. Apollo punished all of Agamemnon's men. Men were dying because Agamemnon had rejected Apollo's priest's pleas.

Apollo's arrows rained down on the Achaeans for nine days. Many men fell. On the tenth day, Achilles spoke to the Achaeans.

"King Agamemnon, I fear we are close to defeat," said Achilles. "The war is almost lost. If we can escape our deaths—which might be hard while Apollo rages against us—we should sail home." The soldiers around Achilles all agreed.

"First, though," Achilles continued, "we need to find out why the god Apollo rages against us. We must set it right."

The wisest of the prophets rose. He was able to see the past, present, and future. The prophet stood beside Achilles and spoke to him.

"Achilles," he said. "I can explain Apollo's anger. I will tell you everything. But you must promise me something first. Swear that you will defend me with all your heart and all your strength. Someone will be angry when I speak the truth. He is a powerful man. He is a king. Think about this carefully, Achilles. Will you stand by me?"

Achilles reassured the prophet. "Be brave! Speak your mind. I swear by Zeus, no one will lay a hand on you while I am alive."

The prophet spoke out bravely. "Beware! Apollo is enraged because King Agamemnon refused to free Chryses's daughter. Apollo will continue to bring us pain until we return the girl to her father. Only then will Apollo forgive us." The prophet sat down.

Agamemnon rose. His eyes were afire with anger. He faced the prophet and gave him a deadly look. "Prophet of misery! It is *my* fault Apollo has turned against us?! All because I refused to give back the girl? Fine! I will give her back if that will stop Apollo's anger and save my people. But I shall not suffer for this. If I must lose my prize, then I must have another."

Achilles answered him quickly. "Agamemnon, how can you receive a prize now? We have no treasure. And we cannot take from the good soldiers who fight for us. Return the girl and we will find a prize for you later. When we destroy Troy, you will receive many prizes."

"Achilles," Agamemnon said. "Are you trying to trick me? You will keep your prize, but must I lose mine? You asked the prophet for an answer. I cannot help it if you do not like my response. I will give back Chryses's daughter to him. And then you will hand over your slave to me."

Agamemnon turned to Odysseus and said to him, "Take Chryses's daughter back to him. Bring a sacrifice for Apollo to calm him."

Achilles became angry. He said to the king, "How dare you! We brave warriors crossed mountains and seas to fight for you and Menelaus. We are your loyal subjects. I fight just as hard as you, maybe even harder. I fight until I am exhausted, and I am happy for the little I receive. How dare you take from your own faithful soldier? And how do we know you won't steal from the rest of us? I am finished! I will go home rather than fight alongside you."

"Desert your post, then! I will find other men to protect and honor me. Of all the generals, I dislike you the most," Agamemnon shouted. "Your slave will be mine. Remember, I am greater and more powerful than you."

Nestor, a general and adviser to the king, stood between the two men. "Please," he said, "do not let your anger take over. We cannot fight each other. We must remember who our real enemy is."

But Achilles considered drawing his sword and killing Agamemnon right then and there.

Agamemnon was his king and his leader, but Achilles was angry. Achilles's hand trembled as he placed it on the handle of his sword. Suddenly the goddess Athena appeared.

Athena said, "Hera sent me because she loves you both. Achilles, Agamemnon—stop this fighting now. I promise that you will be rewarded later. You will be rewarded more than you can imagine."

"I cannot disobey you or Hera," Achilles said. He took his hand from his sword. "But I will never follow Agamemnon again," he said. "I am done fighting his wars."

Achilles left Agamemnon's camp. His soldiers and Patroclus, his closest friend, followed him. He did not turn back to look at Agamemnon. Nor did he watch as Odysseus left with his cargo. The rage of Apollo would soon be over, but the rage of Achilles was just beginning.

CHAPTER 2

Achilles Weeps

King Agamemnon sent two men to Achilles's camp to take his slave. He did not feel guilty about this. Agamemnon did not think he was doing anything wrong. As king, he thought he should get anything he wanted. If someone disagreed, he was being disloyal. Achilles therefore deserved to lose his slave to satisfy the king.

"If he won't give her to you," Agamemnon told his men, "tell him I will go myself and take her by force."

The two men were not happy about their

task but were loyal to their king. They feared Achilles's anger. When they arrived at Achilles's camp, they did not have to speak. Achilles knew why they were there. He put the men at ease.

"Do not be afraid," Achilles said. "I do not blame you. Sit down and have dinner with us. Let us not fight."

Achilles, Patroclus, and the two men enjoyed a large meal inside his tent. They ate, drank, and told stories of battles they had fought together. It was a short break during a difficult time. When the meal was over, Achilles stood up and walked to the entrance.

"Take what you came for," he said. He asked Patroclus to get his slave.

"But remember that you are taking from me—a friend and fellow soldier," he said to the men. "While gods and mortals watch, a ruthless king takes what is not his. King Agamemnon is making a grave mistake."

Achilles watched as the men took his slave. They walked her along the shore, back to King Agamemnon's camp.

Achilles wept angry tears. He left his camp to walk by himself. He sat down beside the sea to think. He prayed to his mother, Thetis, a goddess of the sea.

"Oh, Mother," he cried aloud. "I have been wronged. I have never been so angry before. It is raging through me. It is filling my eyes with tears. I have been cheated. I need revenge!"

Achilles's noble mother heard him weeping. She rose from the sea and sat down beside him. Thetis stroked his head gently and whispered his name. "Achilles, my child, tell me what troubles you."

"Mother! Agamemnon disgraces me, but Zeus and the gods do nothing. My own soldiers do nothing!"

Achilles told his mother what had happened

between him and the king. "I have always been loyal to my king. I never questioned him or his plans. But Apollo was punishing us all for the actions of Agamemnon. And now I must pay twice!"

He then added, "Mother, I want revenge on Agamemnon for his cruelty. Please tell Zeus about my troubles. You have often said that Zeus owes you a favor. You rescued him once when other gods tried to imprison him."

Thetis spoke gently. "What should I ask of Zeus? How can he help you take revenge against Agamemnon?" She stroked his hair as she spoke. She had never seen her son so angry. He was shaking with rage.

"Ask Zeus to aid the Trojans in battle," Achilles said. "I want Agamemnon to know he made a mistake by mistreating me. I am his greatest warrior. He should not disgrace me in front of the whole army."

"Oh, my son," Thetis said. She held his hand and looked into his eyes. Like any mother, Thetis wanted to protect her child. She thought about all the Achaeans who fought with Agamemnon against the Trojans. If all-powerful Zeus sided with the Trojans—even for a short while—many Achaeans could be hurt. Agamemnon was proud. If he did not admit his error quickly, many of his soldiers might die. However, Thetis knew she had only one choice. She loved her son most of all. And his feud with Agamemnon meant Achilles would stay away from the battlefield for a few days more.

"I will go to Olympus and plead your case to Zeus," she said. "Stay here and do not fight in Agamemnon's battles. I will return as quickly as I possibly can."

Thetis left her son to go to Mount Olympus to see Zeus. Achilles sat alone by the sea until darkness fell.

CHAPTER 3

Thetis Pleads for Her Son

ᥣᢦ

Meanwhile, Odysseus arrived at the island where Chryses lived. Odysseus and his men unloaded the Achaeans' sacrifice for Apollo. The lovely daughter of Chryses stepped off the ship. The old priest was overjoyed to hold his daughter in his arms again.

As Odysseus and his men prepared their sacrifice, the priest stretched out his arms and raised them to heaven. "Hear me now, Apollo! End your battle with the Achaeans!"

Then everyone on the island enjoyed a feast.

The men poured drops of wine on the ground to honor the gods. They sang songs praising the gods. Apollo heard the prayers and saw the Achaeans' gifts to him. He was pleased. He ended his storm of arrows over the Achaean camps.

The next morning Odysseus and his men set sail back to King Agamemnon's ships. They left at dawn while the sky was still rosy pink. Apollo provided a strong wind to make their journey easier.

Despite the passing of days, Achilles was still filled with rage. He stayed in his camp with his ship anchored near the shore. He could stand on the deck of his ship to see Agamemnon's ships. But Achilles did not talk to the other generals or his old friends. Only his friend Patroclus stayed by his side.

Meanwhile, when Thetis arrived at Mount Olympus, she found Zeus sitting by himself. She knelt before him and placed her hand on his knee.

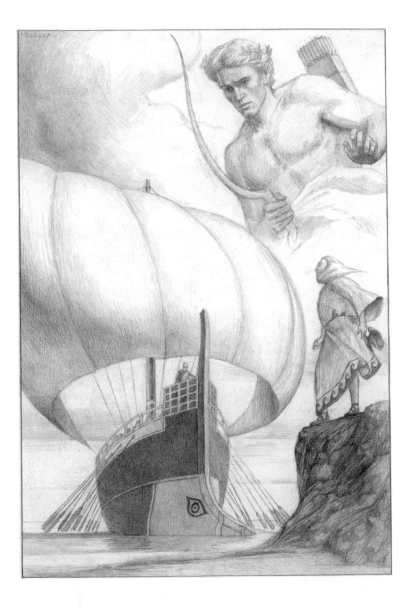

"Lord Zeus, please hear my son's prayer," she said. "Agamemnon has disgraced Achilles." Thetis told Zeus the story of Achilles and Agamemnon. She pointed out that the king was not treating his subjects fairly. "Zeus, I know that you would always be fair to your subjects," she said.

"What would you like from me?" Zeus asked. He spoke gently. He had always liked the noble sea goddess Thetis.

"We ask that you help the Trojans fight against the Achaeans," she said, "until Agamemnon respects my son and gives him the honor he deserves."

Zeus was not pleased with this request. He stood up from his chair and raised his voice in anger. "This is not a simple request! You know this will cause trouble among the gods."

"I only ask for my son," Thetis said calmly.

"This will drive me into a war with my wife,

Hera. She favors the Achaean army and will be very angry if I help the Trojans. She hates the Trojans since Paris chose Aphrodite in that silly contest," he thundered.

Zeus sat back down in his chair. "You saved me once, so I owe you this favor," he said. "I give you my promise. I will help Achilles by favoring the Trojans in battle. But leave me now."

Thetis returned to the sea, and Zeus returned to the great hall of the gods. The gods rose when Zeus arrived, then returned to their seats. Only Hera suspected that something was wrong. She knew Zeus was forming a plan.

She sat on the throne beside him. "What are you up to?" she asked. Zeus did not reply.

Hera's anger was growing. "I know that Thetis came to see you. I assume she asked for a favor for her son. I know that he is angry with his king." Zeus still refused to speak to or look at his wife.

Hera spoke in a harsh whisper. Her voice was almost a hiss. "If you plan to punish the Achaeans to help Achilles, I will make disaster happen. Athena and I will never let the Trojans win. You will only cause more pain and suffering among the mortals if you side with the Trojans. You have my word!"

Zeus ignored his wife's comments. He had already made his decision. He had honored Thetis's request. The matter was settled.

CHAPTER 4

Paris and Menelaus Duel

୬

Agamemnon awoke early. He was ready to attack Troy that very day. Zeus had appeared to him in a dream the night before. The god had told him the time was right to strike. Agamemnon got out of bed, put on his bronze battle armor, and strapped his silver sword over his shoulder. At dawn, King Agamemnon called all his men to gather around him.

The earth rumbled as soldiers responded to Agamemnon's call. The troops rushed from their tents, winding around campfires and across the field. They gathered before their king.

Agamemnon stood before the men. "This war has been full of struggles and disappointments. We have won battles. We have lost men along the way. But we have fought together, side by side," he said. "It will be difficult without Achilles. But we are strong together."

He continued. "Get ready. Polish your armor, sharpen your spears. We will face our enemy with strength and bravery." The men let out a mighty cry, loud enough to rock the waves in the sea. Each man offered something—however small—to the gods. They would be ready for their battle with the Trojan army.

In the city of Troy, the Trojan warriors also prepared for battle. King Priam was too old to fight. Prince Hector, Priam's son and Paris's older brother, led the army.

Hector stood before the men. "Our enemy approaches! After many years of fighting, they are now almost at our city walls. But they will not pass through these gates. They will never take our city!" The soldiers picked up their shields. They raised their swords and spears to salute Prince Hector and King Priam.

The Trojan army flung open the gates of the city, rushing out with a tremendous roar.

The Achaeans moved inland from the shore and their ships. The two armies met on a large open field a few miles from Troy. Paris stepped out of the crowd.

Paris was a handsome man. He looked like a god in his bright bronze armor. He carried a bow and arrow on his back and a sword at his hip. Paris strode to the front line.

Menelaus's chariot was at the front of the Achaean army. He stared at the man who had stolen his wife nine years before. "This is my

chance," he thought. "Paris is now right in front of me. I will get my revenge." Menelaus leaped from his chariot and said, "I will accept your challenge, Paris! Fight me face to face."

Paris became nervous. He stepped backward into the crowd of his army. Magnificent, brave Paris hid from Menelaus.

His brother Hector yelled at him: "Paris, our prince of beauty! You have stolen another man's wife and started a war between countries. Yet you run from a fight. You are a coward! You stole Helen away from Menelaus, and now you cannot face him?"

Paris replied, "Hector, I deserve all the words you have just said. Your words are tough, but they are true. Order both armies to lay down their weapons. Let Menelaus and I face each other alone. We will fight each other for Helen. Whoever wins will have her. Then we can end this war and all live in peace."

Hector rejoiced at his brother's words. He headed toward the Achaean army and told them Paris's challenge.

Menelaus spoke up. "This will not be enough! So many have already suffered because of Paris's actions. But," he said, considering his next words, "I will agree to this if it means peace."

Both sides rejoiced, hoping this truly would mean an end to the long war. They laid their armor down. King Priam was summoned from his palace. He headed outside the city's walls to where the armies stood.

Meanwhile, Helen waited in Troy. She sat in her room, quietly weaving a dark, blood-red tapestry. It showed the Trojans and Achaeans and all they had suffered because of her. Many battles had been fought. So many men had died.

Iris, the messenger of the gods, visited Helen and whispered in her ear: "Come quickly, Helen. See what wondrous things the armies are doing.

They stand in silence, side by side. Paris and Menelaus will fight to end the war. It is all for you. Whoever wins will call you wife!"

Helen's heart filled with sadness. She had fond memories of Menelaus—even though she had not seen him for many years. She did not want him or his men to suffer. And she loved Paris and her family in Troy. She also did not want any of them to suffer. Helen was worried and concerned for both sides.

Helen rushed out of her room with tears in her eyes. A chariot took her to the battlefield.

Kings Priam and Agamemnon met on the field amid all the soldiers standing in silence. Paris and Menelaus stood by their sides.

"Let us agree on the rules of this fight," Agamemnon said. "If Paris wins, the Achaeans will sail home. If Menelaus wins, Paris releases Helen and her riches. No matter who wins, we will declare peace between our armies."

"I can agree to those rules," King Priam said. "But I cannot watch my son fight. I will return to the city knowing that he will win this match." With that, Priam returned to his palace.

Hector and Odysseus marked the field for battle. Paris and Menelaus prepared themselves for the fight. They fastened their helmets and secured their sturdy shields. Then they stood at opposite ends of the field. When the signal was given, they marched toward the middle.

Suddenly, Paris hurled his spear. It hit Menelaus's shield with a loud clang. Then Menelaus pitched his spear. It sank deep into the ground beside Paris. And so the fighting began.

Menelaus lunged at Paris. He grabbed Paris's helmet and dragged him across the field.

The strap on Paris's helmet cut at his throat. Paris could not breathe. He thrashed in panic. He was choking. Menelaus was close to victory.

Then the goddess Aphrodite stepped in. She

had been watching the battle from high up on Mount Olympus. Aphrodite favored the Trojans. She adored Paris.

The goddess snapped the strap of Paris's helmet. Menelaus saw the empty helmet in his fist. He lunged again, but Aphrodite snatched Paris away.

This was easy work for a goddess. She wrapped Paris in swirls of mist and carried him back to Troy. She set him down gently in his bedroom in the palace. Aphrodite traveled back to the battlefield to Helen's side. She said to Helen, "Paris is calling for you. Go back to the palace."

Helen recognized the goddess at once. "Aphrodite, I remember the last time I followed you. You put a spell on me. I left my home with Menelaus and came to Troy. Are you trying to put a spell on me again?" Helen asked. "Are you angry because Menelaus was about to defeat your handsome Paris?"

Aphrodite replied, "Don't anger me, Helen. Remember, I am a goddess. I can ruin you!"

So Helen followed Aphrodite to Paris's bedroom. "Here you are, husband, returned from battle. I have boasted for so many years about how you are a better man than Menelaus. Why not go back now and finish your fight? Or maybe you are afraid he will kill you!"

Paris replied, "Do not insult me or my courage. Menelaus has won today. But I shall crush him tomorrow."

Helen sat down beside her husband. She still felt sad, but she loved Paris. She decided she would stick by him during the war.

Back on the battlefield, Agamemnon and the Achaeans celebrated. "We have won!" the king said. "It is clear that the victory goes to Menelaus. Aphrodite took Paris just as he was about to lose. Now we have a truce between us. The war is over!"

CHAPTER 5

The Battle Begins Again

⌒

Zeus and the gods sat on Mount Olympus. They discussed the mortals.

"I believe the victory goes to Menelaus," Zeus said. "But Aphrodite pulled Paris away before the fight was done. Maybe Paris would have won the battle if he had stayed."

As Zeus spoke, the goddesses Athena and Hera whispered. They were plotting the destruction of Troy.

Hera shouted at Zeus. "Why did you try to help Achilles? Athena and I have worked hard to make sure the city of Troy falls. But you have gotten in the way! Now all our hard work is ruined."

Zeus replied, "I honor Troy as much as you hate it. The Trojans have always honored me."

"I will prove you wrong," Hera said. "Send Athena down to earth. She will see that the Trojans are ready to break the truce with the Achaeans."

Athena dropped to the earth in a flash of light, landing in the middle of the armies. It looked like an explosion. Both sides were confused and frightened. Was the battle on again? Both armies thought that the other army was starting to attack again.

Hector acted quickly. He ordered the Trojans to make the first move.

His soldiers ran across the field toward the Achaeans and attacked. They threw their spears and swung their swords. One of the best Trojan archers took aim at Menelaus. His arrow flew swiftly through the crowd and struck Menelaus. The great general fell to the ground. King Agamemnon rushed to his side.

"Brother, do not die here," Agamemnon said. "You must live! The Trojans broke the truce. We cannot let them win now. The Trojans wronged you, my brother, by stealing your wife. They must pay for their actions!"

"Have courage," Menelaus said. "Don't alarm the men. The wound is not deep. My armor stopped the arrow. It won't be long before I am well again." Agamemnon dragged Menelaus off the battlefield so that a healer could help him.

The Trojans continued their attack. The Achaeans fought back, but they were getting tired. They truly wanted to go home. After the truce, they had lost their fighting spirit.

The Achaeans started to blame King Agamemnon for their troubles. Until this point, they had been slowly but steadily winning the battles. They should not have rushed the gates of Troy so soon. The Achaean army was not prepared for this face-to-face battle.

The Aechaeans faced many obstacles. The Trojans were fighting in their homeland. They were more familiar with the land than the Achaeans. Also, men from nearby regions came out to support the Trojans. They all fought together under Hector's leadership.

The two armies clashed. They raised their swords and shields. Soldiers on both sides fell to the ground. There were many losses.

But Diomedes, an Achaean general, had not lost his fighting spirit. He fought many Trojans that day. He shouted at his enemies as he attacked. "I will not retreat!" he yelled.

Diomedes prayed to Athena, the goddess of war. "Give me the strength of the gods to fight our enemies," he called. "Give me special sight to see who is a man and who is a god. With my new strength I will fight anyone I find on the battlefield. I will fight, and I will win." Athena granted his wish.

Then Aeneas stepped onto the battlefield. He was a Trojan hero and the son of Aphrodite. He attacked Diomedes and let out a bloodcurdling cry as he swung his sword.

Diomedes quickly jumped out of the way. He lifted a giant boulder over his head. Normally, it would take two men to lift a boulder that size. But Diomedes lifted it with ease. He threw the boulder at Aeneas and hit the Trojan's leg. Aeneas fell with a cry.

Aphrodite swept in once again. She stood in front of her wounded son, shielding him.

Aeneas tried to get up, but the whole world went black as night. Aphrodite picked him up in her arms and tried to carry him away.

Diomedes lunged at the goddess. He stabbed her wrist with his spear.

Aphrodite screamed. She was both shocked and hurt. No human had ever attacked a god before. In her pain, Aphrodite dropped her son on the ground. But Aeneas did not stay there for long.

Apollo swooped down and picked up Aeneas. He covered himself and Aeneas in a swirling dark mist to keep them safe from flying arrows.

Aphrodite flew away from the battlefield. She was in agony—frightened and in pain. She found Ares, the god of war, resting on a cloud. She showed Ares her wound. He was enraged.

"I have stayed away from this war for many years," Ares said. "I did not want to get involved. But I cannot allow this injustice! No mortal shall wound a god and get away with it." Ares was a powerful and dangerous god. "I will teach those Achaeans a lesson," he said.

Ares came down to earth on his chariot. He disguised himself as a human and stood next to Hector. The god whispered in the Trojan prince's ear. He gave the mortal the strength to push the Achaean army away from Troy.

But Athena had answered Diomedes's prayers. He could see the gods on the battlefield despite their disguises. Diomedes saw Ares advising Hector. He immediately knew that his army was in trouble. Only Zeus was more powerful on the battlefield than Ares.

The gods watched the action from Mount Olympus. They were excited by the battles and wanted to join in. One by one, all the gods and goddesses swooped down to join the battle between the Trojans and the Achaeans.

But Diomedes was fierce, too. He fought every human and god who came his way. He was brutal and fearless in his attack. And Athena was there to protect him.

"You have nothing to fear," Athena told Diomedes. "I am standing with you. Hera supports you, too."

The words of Athena encouraged Diomedes. He stepped forward and moved toward Ares. The Achaean soldier faced the god of war.

"Do you really think you are as strong as a god?" Ares said. "You will never win, no matter what Athena promised you."

"You do not frighten me," Diomedes said. "And you will not defeat me."

Diomedes lunged toward Ares. The two struggled for some time, mortal man against immortal god.

"I feel sorry for you," Ares mocked. "You are trying so hard, but it will never be enough."

"You think you know everything because you are a god," Diomedes replied. "But you cannot truly see me. You cannot see how strong I am. I will never give up!"

Ares swept his sword toward Diomedes. The Achaean warrior jumped out of the way. One blow after another was met with a shield or a dodge. Neither man nor god backed down. Even though he was fighting a god, Diomedes was not tired. With every move, he felt stronger because the goddess Athena never left his side.

Diomedes stabbed Ares with his sword. Athena held Ares still while Diomedes pushed the sword farther into the god.

Ares cried out in pain. Everyone on the battlefield stopped for a moment. They all watched as Ares jumped into his chariot and flew back to Mount Olympus.

Ares fumed in anger. But his stab wound healed quickly. That was the beauty of being a god. Only the mortal men on the battlefield were left with fatal injuries. Ares relaxed in the great hall after a hard day's battle.

Achilles, too, was resting at his camp. But he was not relaxed. He was still angry with King Agamemnon. But he was safe and far from the battle.

CHAPTER 6

Hector Returns to Troy

༄

All the gods had gone back to Mount Olympus. But the war between the Achaean and Trojan armies continued. The armies moved across the battlefield. The soldiers stabbed everywhere with bronze lances. The sound of swords clanging ripped through the air. But the action was slowly moving closer and closer to the walls of Troy.

Zeus sent Iris, the messenger goddess, to Hector. She ordered him back to Troy. "Tell your mother to gather the older noble women and enter Athena's shrine. They need to pray and ask for mercy for the women and children of Troy. Diomedes must not enter Troy. He is a madman and is now the strongest Achaean. The gods have all left the battlefield. It is only man against man now. Even the gods fear Diomedes since he injured Ares."

Hector returned to his city. He found his mother, Queen Hecuba, in the palace. She was surprised to see him.

"My child, why have you come home?" she said as she hugged him.

"We are losing ground, Mother," Hector said. "The Achaeans are pushing us back to the city walls. You must prepare in case they push through the gates. You must pray for the Trojan army. Go to Athena's temple. Gather the other noble women and go with offerings,"

His mother did as he asked. She gathered many Trojan women to join her in Athena's temple. The women all prayed for Trojan success in the war against the Achaeans. They knew that Achilles was the most feared Achaean warrior, and so they asked Athena to save them from him in particular. They hoped that their prayers would persuade Athena to end her loyalty to the Achaeans. But the goddess refused to hear their prayers.

While the women prayed, Hector went to find his brother Paris. He found him in his bedroom, polishing his battle gear.

"What are you doing?" Hector yelled at his brother. "Our people are dying all around us! And they are dying in battle to defend you! But you are here, safe in your bedroom and cleaning your armor? You must rejoin our people to defend yourself and our city."

Handsome Paris replied, "Hector, you blame me fairly. I deserve it all. I have been cowardly for too long. Please hear me, though. I am not hiding from anyone anymore. I was terribly upset after my fight with Menelaus. But my good wife, Helen, has repaired my spirits. She reminded me that we Trojans can win this war. She has inspired me to join the battle again. You lead, brother, and I will follow you."

Hector shook his brother's hand. "That's what I wanted to hear. I will lead you back to the battlefield. First I must find my wife. I want to see her before heading back into battle."

Hector searched the streets of Troy. He found his wife and infant son at the city's gates. His wife ran to meet him, holding the baby.

"Darling husband," she cried. "Give up this battle! Stay with us and protect the city. The Achaeans are getting closer. We need you here."

Hector kissed her. "I am a general, but I am also a soldier," he said. "I must fight with my army."

He kissed his wife again and then kissed his son. He bid them good-bye. Then he walked through the gates toward the battlefield. His family returned home.

Hector saw his brother approaching the gates. Paris was dressed in his armor and was ready for battle. He noticed that Hector was moving quite slowly.

"Why so slow, brother?" he asked. "You told me to be quick. Yet you linger."

Hector shook his head and said, "My wife just pleaded with me to give up the fight. But I had to say good-bye to her and my baby son. Forgive me if I linger for a moment." Hector sighed heavily. He collected his emotions. "But I am ready now. It is time for battle."

Hector walked through the gate, and Paris followed. They were both eager to rejoin the battle. When they got to the battlefield, they found that the fighting had not slowed down while they were away.

The Trojan forces gained strength when

Hector and Paris returned. The soldiers fought harder with their leaders there. But Hector could see that his men were exhausted.

Hector stepped forward and challenged the most skilled Achaean to fight. He wanted to get rid of their best warrior. "Let us fight to the death," Hector said to the enemy army, sure he would win. "The winner keeps the loser's armor but not his body. We must be allowed to bury our own dead."

King Agamemnon agreed to the terms. Ajax, one of his ablest generals, stepped forward to fight Hector.

The two soldiers clashed in the middle of the battlefield. Their swords swung and slashed. Their shields blocked the stabs and slashes. Each man fell to the ground more than once, their knees buckling after a strong blow. Athena and Apollo sat at the top of an oak tree. They silently watched the action below.

Suddenly, two messengers from Mount Olympus appeared on the battlefield. They stood between Ajax and Hector and stopped the fighting. "Zeus has sent us. He wants the fighting to stop. Nighttime has arrived. It is time for rest," one said.

"Yes," Hector agreed. "The gods have spoken. Let us have time to rest and to bury our dead."

Agamemnon stepped forward. "Agreed. We will go back to our camps. You will go back to yours. Celebrate your brave warriors and pray to your gods. We will fight again tomorrow."

Apollo and Athena returned to Mount Olympus. They knew there would be no more fighting that day. The mortals left the battlefield as darkness fell.

CHAPTER 7

The Scales of Fate

The next morning, Zeus gathered all the gods at the bottom of Mount Olympus.

"You know I have witnessed all that has happened. You gods have interfered too much in this war. You must not involve yourselves in these mortal matters. I am the only one who can control this war.

"No god or goddess may act against my strict orders," Zeus continued. "Obey me now so I can bring this war to a swift end. If I catch any immortal acting against my orders, I will bring you back to Mount Olympus and punish you. I will make sure you are eternally disgraced. Do not doubt how powerful I am. I am Zeus, king of the gods!"

All the gods and goddesses were speechless. They had heard the word of Zeus loud and clear.

Finally Athena rose and spoke. "Zeus, you are high and mighty! We already know your power is great. Who can stand against you? We pity these warriors. They live only so that they may die brutally. But we will keep out of their war, as you command. We will only offer advice to the Trojans and Achaeans. Perhaps we can save some of their lives this way."

Zeus nodded and climbed aboard his chariot. He put on his armor and picked up his whip. His bronze-hoofed horses raced the wind. Their golden manes flowed behind them. He rode to the peak of Mount Olympus. He unleashed his horses and then sat on his throne. There he could watch over all of the heavens and Earth, the city walls of Troy, the battlefields and camps, and even the Achaean warships anchored offshore.

And on Earth, the Trojans and Achaeans put their armor on. They were set to fight once again. The gates of Troy were flung wide open, and the Trojan army poured out. Horses, chariots, and soldiers advanced. A tremendous roar went up to the heavens as the two armies met again for battle.

The Trojans and Achaeans clashed again. They slammed their shields. They swung their spears and swords. Men fought hand to hand. The thunder of their struggle roared and rocked the earth. The deathly screams mingled with triumphant cries. Fighters killed, and other fighters were killed.

The battle lasted all morning. At noon, Zeus stood at his scale. Today, he would let the fates decide. He carefully weighed the fates of both armies. The Achaean army's fate sank low. The fate of the Trojans lifted toward the sky. Zeus sent a thunderbolt down into the middle of the battle. It crashed into the Achaean army. Some of the soldiers fell. A hot terror seized them all.

Agamemnon and Ajax were pushed back from the battlefield. Even brave Odysseus ran away. The Achaeans ran from the battlefield back to their camps. They moved closer to the ships so they could escape, if necessary. Diomedes could not believe it.

"Odysseus, come back here! You are a coward. Come back and join me to take down these Trojans!" Diomedes shouted in Odysseus's direction. But Odysseus did not hear him. He had run too far away.

Nestor, the old and wise commander, did not run. He and his men attached their team of horses to Diomedes's team. The men fearlessly shot their spears at the Trojans.

Another thunderbolt hit. This time it landed at Diomedes's feet. It struck the earth in a blinding, smoking flash. Nestor realized what they were up against. He called to Diomedes. "Quick, turn the horses around! Zeus is against us today. It looks like he is giving today's victory to the Trojans."

"You are right, old friend," Diomedes said. "But I cannot run away from battle. I cannot give Hector that satisfaction. I would rather the earth swallowed me whole."

"But everyone has seen how powerful you are," Nestor shouted to him. "Give up for today! I beg you. Zeus is against us. We will not win if we keep fighting."

Diomedes gave in to his wise friend's request. They turned their chariots around. They raced back toward their ships, which were waiting for them on the shores near Troy.

As Diomedes and Nestor raced away, they

could hear the Trojans shouting after them. They called them cowards and quitters.

Diomedes was tempted to go back. But as he began to turn, Zeus let loose another thunderbolt at his feet. Diomedes pointed his chariot back in the direction of his army's ships. All the Achaeans were retreating.

Hector gave a mighty roar to all the Achaean men leaving the battlefield. "Look," he shouted. "Zeus favors us! He grants me glory and gives you a bloody death. Nothing can hold me back now! When my Trojan army reaches your ships, we will set them on fire. We will steal Nestor's golden shield and Diomedes's armor! We will take all—tonight!"

Hector roared and bragged. Hera heard him and was outraged. She shook in her throne so violently that Mount Olympus quaked. She called to Poseidon, the god of the sea. "Poseidon! We have heard nothing from you during this war. Can't you see what your brother Zeus has done? He favors the Trojans and punishes the Achaeans. Do you have no pity for the Achaean men who are dying? They offer you sacrifices and honor. Will you leave them to die?"

Poseidon replied, "Hera, this is not the time for me to get involved. This is not my battle. I am powerful but do not want to cross Zeus. He is too strong. He can crush us all. As long as the Achaeans are strong and have a chance of winning, I will keep my distance."

Hector and his army pushed on in the direction of the Achaean ships. The Trojans were forceful. They were ready to conquer all. But Hera's will was strong, and she wanted the Achaeans to win. The goddess whispered into King Agamemnon's ear. She encouraged him to push his army to fight back.

"Don't give up!" she said. "You must lead your men. Bring them back into battle."

The king called out to his men. "Stay strong, brave soldiers! The gods have not forgotten us!"

When his men were out of earshot, Agamemnon prayed to Zeus. "Zeus, why do you strike against us? I have always made sacrifices to you. If you will do nothing else, please let my men escape with their lives. Don't let the Trojans mow us all down."

Agamemnon watched his men on the battlefield. He could still feel Hera's support. But he knew they would lose this war if Zeus did not take pity on them.

CHAPTER 8

Hera and Athena Make a Plan

∽

Zeus was moved by Agamemnon's words. He decided to take pity on the Achaeans.

Zeus sent an eagle flying over the head of King Agamemnon. The eagle carried a young deer in its claws. The eagle dropped the deer right in front of the Achaeans. The deer was alive, and it ran off into the distance. The Achaeans knew this was a positive sign from Zeus.

Agamemnon addressed his men. "You have all seen this sign. Zeus sent us an eagle. He is with us today. Diomedes, you will lead us into battle. All the Achaeans will follow our strongest warrior to victory!"

The soldiers' strength and courage were renewed. They charged back toward the Trojans with force. Diomedes led the way. The whole Achaean army followed.

Teucer, an Achaean archer, sent an arrow flying through the air toward Hector. He missed but hit one of Hector's brothers. Teucer shot another arrow at Hector but missed again. This time he hit Hector's chariot driver. The driver fell off the chariot onto the ground. The chariot's horse stumbled and almost fell, too. Hector jumped from his chariot. He sent a mighty yell ringing through the air.

Hector grabbed a rock and threw it at Teucer just as the archer let another arrow fly. The rock hit Teucer on the collarbone. He dropped to his knees, stunned. Ajax ran to Teucer's side and protected him with his shield.

Hector's anger was at full power. He let his army show the Achaeans how powerful it was. The Trojans took down soldier after soldier from the Achaean army. They pushed back their enemy. The Trojans began to win again.

Hera saw the Trojan side gaining strength. Her anger boiled again. She called to Athena. "Are we going to let this happen?" she asked. "This is our last chance. I cannot bear to watch this maniac Hector defeat the Achaeans!"

Athena agreed. "How can Zeus allow this? I have done so many favors for him. But now he just leaves the Achaeans to be crushed by the Trojans. And all this because Thetis cried that her son, Achilles, needed help."

Athena and Hera had had enough. They put their armor on and got their horses ready. They rushed out of the gates to join the war.

But Zeus sees all. He knew that Athena and Hera were disobeying him. Zeus sent a messenger to stop the goddesses from joining the war again. "They must not go against me on this matter," he warned. "Tell them they will suffer."

The messenger rushed to find Athena and Hera. She met the goddesses close to the gates of Troy. "Zeus forbids you to take action in the Achaeans' name. He promises severe punishment if you continue."

Hera turned to Athena. She felt defeated. "We must be careful," Hera said to Athena. "We cannot risk so much for mortal men. We must let Zeus decide their fates." Hera and Athena turned to go back to Mount Olympus.

When the goddesses returned to the great hall, Zeus mocked them. "Why do you both look so sad? Are you tired from trying to join the mortals in battle?" he joked.

Then Zeus turned serious. "If you had decided to interfere, neither of you would be allowed back on Mount Olympus again."

Hera and Athena whispered to each other behind Zeus's back. Maybe they were forbidden to join in the battle. But they could still plot the end of Troy. They could still find a way to support the Achaean army.

Back on the battlefield, night was falling. Hector knew he had to end the battle for the day even though his army had such great energy. He delivered a fiery speech to his troops to keep up their fighting spirit.

"We are closer than ever, my friends! Zeus is on our side. But we must go back to camp for now. Rest up tonight. We will defeat the Achaeans tomorrow! We will either destroy them or send them running from Troy once and for all!"

CHAPTER 9

A Plea to Achilles

The Trojans spent the night in good spirits. But the Achaeans were overcome by panic. They had lost too much ground in the day's battle. The Achaeans felt like their hearts were breaking. Their grief was overwhelming.

Agamemnon gathered his men and tried to lift their spirits. It was not an easy task, especially because they all felt so low.

"Men, I have been led astray," Agamemnon said. "Zeus promised me long ago that my army would not go home until we crushed Troy. I see now that it was all a trick. Now he commands that we return home in disgrace. He wants many of our men to lose their lives. Zeus is too powerful. We cannot fight against him. So listen to me—leave now! We will never take the broad streets of Troy."

Agamemnon's men were silent for a long time. They did not know what to do. Everyone wondered if this was another trick.

Finally, Diomedes spoke. "I will be the first to oppose you, King! Spare me your anger. You have called me a coward before. I do not care what you think. You have a throne and you have a crown. But you do not have courage.

"And to my fellow soldiers—if your spirit drives you to go home, then sail away! You are not meant for battle. But the rest of us will continue. We will fight until we have ruined Troy. Even if there are only two men left. We will fight, and we will win! Never forget—we all sailed here with the gods on our side."

Nestor stood up. "I am old and have much experience," he said. "I agree with Diomedes. King, put out a feast for your men tonight. Serve fine food and drink. This is what your men need right now. This is the night that will make or break our army. Either we will crumble tomorrow or we will pull through. Now is the time to unite and strengthen our troops.

"And I will remind you of this: our downfall began when you fought with Achilles. You dishonored a man whom the gods favor. This is why we have trouble now. Let us bring Achilles back in friendship."

"That is no lie, old man," Agamemnon quickly agreed. "We are in trouble because I fought with Achilles. We are at a loss without him. Achilles is the bravest and best warrior. He could fight an entire army on his own. I will do anything to regain his friendship." Agamemnon listed all the riches he would give to Achilles. He even said he would return Achilles's slave.

Odysseus and Ajax led a group of men to deliver the news to Achilles.

They found the brave warrior at his camp near his ship. Achilles was surprised to see his old friends. He greeted them warmly and welcomed them to his camp.

"Come, Odysseus! Come, Ajax! Enter my tent," Achilles said. "Patroclus, please help me welcome our friends. There should be a cup in everyone's hand. We all must dine, talk, and laugh together. For here are some of the men I love the most. I have missed them." Patroclus ordered a festive meal to be brought to them.

Odysseus and Ajax gave Achilles an update about the war. It had been only a few days, but so much had happened.

"Now Hector waits for dawn to arrive so he

can attack," Odysseus said. "It will be our fate to die in Troy, far from home." He looked out over the sea into the distance.

"But King Agamemnon has sent us with a message of peace," Ajax added. "He sends his apologies and admits that he was wrong. Agamemnon made a promise to give gifts to you. He will even give back your slave, which he admits he stole. We need you, Achilles. We cannot win this war without you."

"I hate that man more than I hate the gates of the underworld," Achilles said. His face was red with anger. "He has embarrassed me in front of the entire Achaean army. He has not led us well through these years of battle. I have risked my life for him many times. Yet he does not truly respect me or any of his men. The king lies as easily as he breathes. I do not trust him.

"We have come here because Helen left her husband for Paris. Does King Agamemnon not understand that other men also love their wives and families?

"Why should I fight for him? He has no sense of reality! It does not matter if you are a coward or if you are brave. The result of joining Agamemnon's battle will be the same: death."

Odysseus tried to speak, but Achilles did not let him, saying, "This is my advice to all Achaean soldiers and generals—sail home now! You will never see the destruction of Troy."

Odysseus and Ajax both tried to persuade Achilles to come back and fight with them. But Achilles would not change his mind. "Unless the Trojans get too close to my ship—and threaten my possessions or my journey home—I will not fight again." Odysseus and Ajax left Achilles's camp without him.

Everyone was waiting for Odysseus and Ajax to return. Agamemnon was anxious for news from Achilles.

Once they returned, Agamemnon asked, "Will he come back and fight with us? Or does his rage still consume him?"

Odysseus replied, "Achilles has no intention of cooling his rage. He's still bursting with anger. He refuses you and all your gifts."

All the Achaean men stood in silence. They were stunned.

Odysseus spoke again. "King, you should never have offered him gifts. Achilles is a proud man. You have only hurt that pride again. I say forget him. He will do what he wants to do. Let us go to sleep now and rise at daybreak. We are the mighty Achaean army. If we are united, we will win!"

The men cheered. They made offerings and sent prayers to the gods. Then they went back to their tents. They spent the night there and took the gift of sleep.

CHAPTER 10

Spies in the Night

~⌒~

But Agamemnon could not sleep. He paced through his camp all night long. The king could see the thousand Trojan campfires in the distance. He was panic-stricken. He knew there was no way his army could win. How *could* they win when Zeus was not on their side? Agamemnon went to talk to Nestor. The old, wise man would have a plan.

On his way to find Nestor, Agamemnon met his brother Menelaus on the shore by the ships. Menelaus was packing and checking equipment.

He was keeping busy. He could not sleep either. There was too much to worry about.

"We will have a plan by the morning," Agamemnon assured his brother. "We will face the Trojans with honor."

The king approached Nestor's tent. When he entered, he found Nestor asleep. Nestor was ready for battle. He was wearing his armor. His shield and sword were within reach.

Nestor woke up suddenly when he heard someone approaching. He jolted upright and shouted, "Who goes there?!"

Agamemnon announced himself at once. He told Nestor why he was visiting.

"Let us gather the generals," Nestor said. "We need to figure out a plan together."

They walked through the camp and woke up the other three generals: Odysseus, Ajax, and Diomedes. The men, including Menelaus, gathered in Agamemnon's tent to talk.

Nestor asked, "Is there someone among us who could spy on the Trojans? Perhaps we could learn their plans for tomorrow morning. The person who could get this information would be greatly celebrated."

Diomedes was the first to respond. "I can do this. But someone else should come with me." Everyone volunteered to go with Diomedes.

King Agamemnon said, "Good Diomedes, thank you for volunteering. This is a dangerous task. Pick your partner and be gone. Choose the person you think is the best."

"If the choice is mine," Diomedes said, "then I must choose Odysseus. He is a very brave man. With him by my side, I could go through fire and still make it back alive."

Odysseus then cut him off. "Let us move, Diomedes. Dawn will arrive soon. We need the information before the morning."

The two men put their battle gear on.

Odysseus grabbed a bow, a quiver of arrows, and a sword. He wore a helmet made of leather. Diomedes took his sword and shield. He wore a brass helmet with a leather strap under his chin. The two men headed out.

Odysseus and Diomedes prayed to Athena to protect them. They made their way toward the Trojan camp like lions on the hunt.

❧

The Trojan leaders were not spending the night sleeping either. Hector also had called a meeting with his generals. He wanted the perfect strategy for reaching and destroying the Achaean ships. He asked for a volunteer to sneak up to the ships. "We need to know how well guarded they are," Hector said.

Dolon, one of Hector's soldiers, accepted the challenge. "But I want the chariot and team of horses that carry great Achilles. If we succeed, that must be my prize."

Hector agreed to those terms. "Once we take down the Achaeans, you will certainly have your prize," he promised.

Dolon headed toward the Achaean camp. He ran quietly along the plain that was the battlefield during the day.

Although Dolon was quiet and covered by the dark night, the keen eye of Odysseus spotted him.

"Who is that man?" Odysseus whispered to Diomedes. "Someone has just left the Trojan camp. Let us hide so he will pass us. Then we can catch him from behind."

The two men lay down quietly on the ground. Dolon passed them. Odysseus and Diomedes sprang up and followed the Trojan soldier. Dolon heard a noise. He stopped moving and turned around. At first Dolon thought it was his own men following him. Perhaps Hector had called off his mission.

But then he realized it was the enemy. He ran fast back toward the Trojan camp.

But he could not get away fast enough. Odysseus was stronger and faster than anyone else. Diomedes kept pace close behind.

Diomedes threw his spear over Dolon's head. The spear hit the ground right at his enemy's feet. The Trojan was forced to stop in his tracks. Odysseus and Diomedes pounced on Dolon and pinned him to the ground.

"Please," Dolon cried, shaking with fear. "Spare me! If you don't kill me, my father will offer you a handsome reward. He has many riches to give."

Odysseus said, "Then tell us the truth. Why are you roaming across the quiet battlefield? Did Hector send you to spy on our ships? Do you have other reasons?"

"I was sent by Hector," Dolon cried. He told the two Achaeans everything. "He promised me

Achilles's stallions. He sent me to see if the ships were guarded. Hector wanted to know if you were planning a quick escape."

"Why would we escape?" Diomedes asked. "We are not cowards."

"What are Hector's plans?" Odysseus asked. He held on to Dolon's arm tightly. "Does he plan to attack our camp early tomorrow?"

Dolon saw that he was in danger and decided to talk. "The Thracians, who are neighbors and friends of Troy, arrived to help. They have a camp nearby. They are not as good soldiers as we are. But they add to our numbers. We will attack by dawn. Hector hoped to surprise and frighten your army when you saw how many men we had."

Dolon told them where the Thracians were camped. Diomedes and Odysseus took Dolon back to their camp as prisoner. Then the two Achaeans snuck off to find the Thracians.

It was easy to slip into the Thracian camp with no one noticing. Diomedes and Odysseus were very quiet and skilled. It did not take long to capture some of the men, including their king. Diomedes and Odysseus brought them all back as prisoners. They told Agamemnon and the generals everything that Dolon had revealed. It seemed like the Achaeans' fortune was returning.

It had been a long night for Diomedes and Odysseus. They were exhausted but excited about the battle to come. They went down to the shore. They prayed to Athena to aid the Achaeans in battle.

Diomedes and Odysseus then stepped into the sea. They dunked their heads under the waves. They washed themselves and prepared themselves for the battle that morning.

CHAPTER 11

The Battle Rages On

༄

Dawn arrived, and the men awoke. The Achaeans dressed for battle and faced the day with bravery and strength. For the first time in a while, they wished to go into battle rather than run home. They felt hopeful from Odysseus's spirited speech the night before.

Agamemnon dressed in magnificent battle armor. The Achaean king picked up his giant shield and placed his sword in its sheath. He looked like a most fearsome warrior.

He shouted words of encouragement to all

the troops as they dressed in their armor. The generals shouted orders for their drivers to keep the horses and chariots in line. The Achaeans had to stay focused to win. They moved in the direction of their enemy.

On the other side of the battlefield, the Trojans prepared themselves. Hector stood before his men, holding his sword high.

"We are blessed by the gods!" he shouted. "We have no fear of failure because the gods will fight with us."

The Trojans cheered. They stamped on the ground and banged their shields.

"Today victory will be ours!" Hector stepped into his chariot and started toward the battle-field. His men followed.

The gods and goddesses sat up on Mount Olympus to watch the battle. By Zeus's order, no one could get involved. Most of them felt anxious. But they did as Zeus commanded.

Zeus sat alone, pleased with his glory and power. The king of the gods watched as the battle began.

And what a brutal battle it was! The two sides fought all morning. Many men fell. At first, many Achaeans were driven to their deaths. The fight began to look hopeless for them.

Then Agamemnon, in his bright armor, jumped forward. He killed one Trojan general. Then he killed the general's aide. Then he moved on to other foes. He fought with a renewed strength and great confidence. Some of his victims pleaded for their lives. But Agamemnon showed no mercy. The Achaeans began to gain ground. They pushed the Trojans back toward their city's gates.

Hector was worried. He saw so many of his men fall at the hands of the Achaeans.

Zeus sent his messenger down to visit Hector. The messenger gave Hector some advice.

"Step back for now. Do not make your full attack until King Agamemnon is wounded," the messenger said. Hector did as he was told. He stepped back from the fight, and he waited. But many of his soldiers still battled the mighty Agamemnon.

Soon enough, Agamemnon was wounded. A Trojan's sword slashed his arm and knocked him to the ground. The king continued to fight, but after a while, the pain was too much. He ran to his chariot and his driver raced back to camp. He needed some time to heal.

Hector saw the Achaean leader leaving the battlefield and ordered his men to attack. He led his Trojan army straight into the enemy's ranks.

Hector expected an easy victory. But his attack did not go as planned. Even though Agamemnon had left, the Achaeans continued to take down the Trojans. The Trojans' enemies did not slow down or lose their spirit.

The great and fearless Diomedes caused the most damage. Diomedes pulled Trojan men from their chariots as they passed. He raced across the battlefield, killing Trojans and ripping their armor from their bodies.

One of Diomedes's spears even hit Hector's helmet. The spear bounced off the headgear, but it shocked the Trojan warrior. Hector decided to move away from the battle. He needed a moment to recover.

Paris had seen Diomedes attack his brother. The Trojan prince was enraged! Paris shot an arrow and hit Diomedes in the foot. The arrow pinned the Achaean's foot to the ground.

Paris jumped in front of his victim. "Aha! My arrow did not miss. If only it had hit higher, it would have done more damage."

"Yes, that was a fine shot," Diomedes said. "But if you are not a coward, you will fight me face to face. This is just a scratch. You have done me almost no harm." Paris did not accept the challenge. Instead, the Trojan prince turned to fight another Achaean soldier in his path.

Odysseus saw that Diomedes was wounded and ran to him. He shielded his friend while he pulled the arrow from his foot. Diomedes then jumped into his chariot and headed back to his camp. He needed some time to heal.

Odysseus was now alone in this part of the battlefield. He wondered whether he should run or stand his ground. He knew that to run would be a cowardly move. Odysseus was not a coward! Trojan men began to approach him. They created a circle around the brave warrior. Odysseus had no choice but to stay and fight.

Odysseus hit and killed many of the Trojans who circled around him. But the group soon overpowered him. One of them stabbed him in the ribs. Odysseus lay on the ground, bleeding, weak, and desperate. He called out for help as loudly as he could. But he was alone. The Trojans prepared to finish him off.

Menelaus heard the distant cries and called to Ajax. "Odysseus is calling for help. He must be desperate and alone. I have never known Odysseus to ask for help. We must save him! We cannot continue this war without him."

Ajax found Odysseus. The brave warrior was hurt and bleeding. But he had picked himself off the ground to continue fighting. Ajax jumped in beside him. They faced the enemy together. At times, Odysseus was so weak that Ajax had to hold him up while fighting. Soon a chariot arrived and took Odysseus to safety.

Ajax stayed behind. He and his men killed as many Trojans as they could.

Achilles and his men were getting ready to leave. He paused to watch the battle from his ship. He could see that the Achaeans were suffering many losses. "They will come asking for me again," he said. "They cannot survive this battle without me."

Achilles was still angry at Agamemnon. But he loved his fellow soldiers too much to stand by and do nothing. Achilles sent Patroclus to find out more. He wanted to know who still lived and who was dead. Patroclus did as his trusted friend asked. He went to shore and ran to the battlefield.

Patroclus found Nestor right away. The old general told Patroclus about all the men who had been hurt and killed. Patroclus was bewildered. These were men he knew well. These were men he had fought alongside for nearly ten years. He felt as if he had lost many brothers.

Patroclus knew that he could stand by no longer. Even if Achilles refused to fight, Patroclus had to return to battle. His army needed him.

CHAPTER 12

Poseidon Joins the Battle

⌒

The Achaeans knew that the Trojans were coming to attack their ships. So they quickly built a wall to protect the vessels, which were their only way home. It was a tall and strong wall. While the battle raged on, the Achaeans did their best to keep the Trojans from breaking through the wall and destroying their ships.

Zeus had brought Hector and his Trojan army to the Achaeans' wall. With the strength of Zeus guiding them, the Trojans pushed past the wall. They climbed over it and broke it down.

Some Achaeans continued to fight on the battlefield while others fought to defend the wall. When Zeus saw how close the Trojans were to the ships, he decided to leave the battle.

Zeus left both armies to fight on their own. He had promised Thetis that he would help the Trojans only so that Agamemnon would regret losing Achilles. The damage to the Achaeans was now done. The Trojans were at the Achaean ships. Agamemnon now fully regretted his mistake. Zeus flew back to Mount Olympus.

But Zeus still had a view of the whole world from his throne. Zeus was always aware of what was happening below.

Poseidon could wait no more. He had listened to the Achaeans' prayers and cries for too long. He was sitting on Mount Olympus, watching the battle. His throne rested beneath the waves of the sea, but he frequently joined the other gods on Mount Olympus for a better view.

Poseidon was Zeus's brother and a mighty, earth-shaking god. He held a powerful staff called a trident. With three giant steps Poseidon reached his chariot and team of horses. He dove down swiftly from Mount Olympus. His horses' golden manes streamed behind them. The sea opened for him as he approached it. As the sea parted, Poseidon and his horses landed under the water. He fed his horses and chained them to the sea rock so they would stay put. Poseidon rose mightily from the sea to urge on the Achaeans.

Poseidon called to Ajax, who was still fighting bravely on the battlefield. "Do not lose your strength!" he cried. He pointed his trident at Ajax and filled the warrior's heart with strength. Poseidon made Ajax's arms, legs, feet, and hands fill with energy and rage.

Ajax felt an earthquake inside him. He ran through the crowds of his fellow soldiers and tried to encourage each man as he passed. But

the soldiers were all tired. They felt defeated. Seeing the crowds of Trojans approaching their ships made them worry and weep. They wanted to give up once and for all.

"If you lose faith now," he called, "we will surely be defeated! This is not the time for worrying. We need to take action. We need to be strong. Before this attack, the Trojans were easily frightened and easily pushed back. They did not attack us with such strength. Now they are at our ships. This is a terrible thing. But we have won many battles before. We will have victory again! But we must not give up!"

Ajax raced toward the shore, and many Achaeans followed. The soldiers stood tall beside Ajax. They formed a wall of men. The Achaeans raised their shields and prepared to meet the enemy face to face and shield to shield.

The Trojans pounded down on them! They moved in tight groups led by Hector. He intended to push through the Achaean army in one charge. The Trojans meant to crush the Achaean soldiers and reach their ships. But the wall of Achaean men would not let them pass.

This was a battle between gods as much as men. Poseidon had dared to get involved in the war even in the face of Zeus's warning. Zeus and Poseidon were now at odds.

As Poseidon hovered above the armies, he saw one of his grandsons struck down by a Trojan soldier. Poseidon felt a new kind of rage that shook his godly self like an earthquake. Now he turned his rage toward Zeus and the Trojans. He put this rage into the heart of Menelaus.

On the battlefield, Menelaus battled viciously with Pisander, another one of King Priam's sons. Pisander cut off the top of Menelaus's helmet. This was too close a strike for Menelaus. He struck Pisander with his sword. The Trojan fell to the ground in a heap.

Menelaus took Pisander's armor as a prize. He growled with rage. "So you think you Trojans will reach our ships?" he shouted. "You think you will defeat us in battle? You think you can avoid death? Zeus is on your side, but we will not back down. We will not be defeated!"

Menelaus was fuming. "You Trojans stole my wife! And now you try to destroy our ships? You dare to attack us? We will fight back, each of us with the strength of ten thousand men!"

The Trojans' good fortune was turning to disaster. Hector was exhausted and frustrated. He finally lost his temper. Hector let out a savage yell. He led the way, and his captains followed close behind. The Achaean ranks yelled back. No one lost his courage. Mighty roars from both armies reached the realm of Zeus, far above them all.

CHAPTER 13

Hector Is Injured in Battle

N estor was helping the wounded men when he heard the battle cries from his fellow Achaeans. He went off to a lookout point above the battlefield to get a better view.

When he arrived, he found a terrible sight. He could not believe the death and destruction spread out before him. So many men—both Achaean and Trojan—lay on the ground. Nestor knew he must go see King Agamemnon. Their army was in serious trouble. It looked like the Trojans were advancing again.

The ships of Agamemnon, Odysseus, and Diomedes were anchored offshore, away from the fighting. The generals were all tending to their battle wounds. They saw Nestor approach and gathered to meet him on the shore.

"Why are you here?" Agamemnon called. "I need you out there in the battlefield to help defend us. The Trojans want to burn our ships to embers."

Diomedes spoke. "I have a plan. If you will all follow me back into battle, I am sure that we will win. We must return despite our wounds. Our men need to see us fighting. Their courage will strengthen once we return. We could stay on the back lines. From there we can encourage our troops."

The generals agreed to go forward with Diomedes's plan. They headed back into battle with Agamemnon in the lead. Along the way, Poseidon whispered to Agamemnon that he should stay strong. "The gods have not forgotten you," Poseidon said. "A time will come when you will defeat Troy."

The generals stepped onto the battlefield. The soldiers cheered to see their leaders return. They immediately fell into line and followed their generals' directions for the battle.

The two armies continued their fierce fighting. Hector and Ajax were still battling each other. The two men had exchanged many blows, but both were still standing. Hector flung his spear and hit Ajax. But the spear bounced off Ajax's bronze breastplate. Ajax threw a rock at Hector. The rock hit Hector in the chest and sent him flying backward. Hector landed hard onto the dirt. His spear fell from his hand.

Many Achaeans then surrounded Hector. They rushed in to finish the kill. But the Trojan generals were too quick. They placed their shields around Hector and protected their leader from a shower of spears. Then they pulled him off the battlefield. They put Hector in a chariot and raced him back to Troy.

The Achaeans saw that Hector was retreating. They felt confident again. The soldiers pressed on. And every Trojan shook with fear.

Apollo found Hector recovering just inside the walls of Troy. Hector was slowly regaining his strength. But he was still weak.

Apollo asked him, "Hector, son of Priam, why so far from your troops? You are sitting here half dead rather than fighting. Has some trouble come your way?"

"Who are you, my lord?" Hector asked. "How dare you tease me? Ajax struck me in the chest. I almost died."

"Have courage, Hector!" Apollo cried. "Do you not recognize me? I, Apollo, have come to fight with you. Together we will push the Achaeans back."

Hector stood up. The words of the god gave him strength. He climbed back onto his chariot and returned to the battlefield. Apollo followed.

The Trojan men cheered when they saw their leader return. They gathered once more around Hector. As a group, they turned back toward the Achaeans and attacked again. They pushed into the Achaean ranks, but the Achaeans held their ground. They blocked all the spears and arrows the Trojans shot at them.

But Apollo sent fear into the hearts of the Achaeans. He made the Trojans fearless attackers. At once, the Trojans swept through many Achaeans. They slew their enemies left and right. While the Trojans ripped off the armor and weapons of the fallen men, the remaining Achaeans struggled to escape.

Hector stood on his chariot and called to his troops. "Now is the time to make for their ships! Leave the armor and weapons and go for the real

prize." His men let out bloodcurdling cries. They chased the Achaeans back to their ships.

Nestor saw the groups of Trojan men racing to his army's ships. The old, wise soldier called to Zeus. "Zeus, if you have ever loved us—if you have ever enjoyed the offerings we gave you— please help us today. Do not let the Trojans get to our ships. Do not let today be the end of us!"

Zeus sent a thunderclap cracking through the sky in response. But the Trojans thought Zeus's thunder was for them. They pushed toward the ships even harder.

But the Achaeans did not back down. They fought the Trojans who were spilling onto their ships. The Achaeans believed they would never stop fighting. And the Trojans fought back, believing they would be victorious that day.

CHAPTER 14

Patroclus Puts on the Armor

Patroclus went to see Achilles when he returned from the battlefield. He needed to tell his dear friend about the destruction he had seen.

"What is wrong?" Achilles asked his friend Patroclus, who was weeping. "What did you see on the battlefield?"

"I cannot describe how terrible it is, my lord," Patroclus said. "Diomedes, Odysseus, and Agamemnon are all injured. The Achaeans have been driven back to the ships. The Trojans are closing in. They will soon destroy the ships and finish our army for good!" Achilles said nothing in reply.

Patroclus looked Achilles in the eye. "Nothing moves you, does it? Your rage still controls you. You cannot see past it." Patroclus was angry.

"I cannot believe that Thetis is your mother or Peleus is your father," he said. "You have none of their strength and courage. You *must* come out and help defend your fellow soldiers."

Achilles finally replied. "Let us put an end to this argument. I cannot go to battle. I swore I would join only when the fighting reached the ships. That is my final word."

"If you will not go to battle, let me go in your place. I will help defend our army and our ships," Patroclus said.

Back at the ships, Ajax and his fellow generals were struggling to keep the Trojans away. Hector had climbed aboard Ajax's ship with some of his best soldiers. He battled Ajax toe to toe while his soldiers took care of Ajax's men. The two mighty generals exchanged fierce blows. Ajax lunged at Hector with his spear. Hector sidestepped and chopped off the top of Ajax's spear with one clean swoop of his sword. He had little hope now for the safety of his ship. He knew that this was the work of the gods.

Trojans on shore set arrows on fire, shooting them at the ships. Ajax's ship went up in flames. Hector and his men quickly left the ship and rowed back to shore, watching it burn.

From his own ship, a few miles out at sea, Achilles saw Ajax's ship burn. At last, he understood why Patroclus had to join the battle.

"Strap on my gear and lead the men," Achilles said to Patroclus with urgency. "If the Trojans see my armor, they will be filled with fear. Go now! We cannot let the rest of the ships burn. Go and strike fear into the hearts of all Trojans."

Patroclus put on his friend's armor and

grabbed his shield. The armor was made of heavy, strong bronze. It was well polished and shone brightly in the strong sunlight. The helmet sat high on the head of Patroclus. Bright red feathers adorned the top. But he did not take Achilles's sword. It was too heavy for anyone but Achilles to lift. Only Achilles was skilled enough to use it.

Patroclus entered the battle with bravery and might. The Trojans were shocked to see the armor. They thought Achilles had returned to battle. Some even tried to run away. These men feared the great Achilles. Patroclus gained strength by wearing Achilles's armor and seeing the Trojans' fear.

He landed a spear and killed a Trojan first thing. Many Achaeans, also thinking Achilles had joined them, followed him. They trapped a troop of Trojans led by Zeus's favorite son, Sarpedon, against one of the ships. They had no place to go and could not make their way back to Troy. Patroclus and the Achaean men mowed down the troop.

Sarpedon was horrified to see so many of his men fall. He leaped from his chariot to the ground, fully armed. Patroclus saw him and jumped down from his chariot, too. They rushed at each other and shouted to the heavens.

Zeus, looking down from his throne, said to Hera: "My cruel fate! The son I love most will soon die at the hands of Patroclus. My heart is torn in two. Shall I pluck him up now, while he's still alive, and set him down someplace safe? Or do I let him find his fate with Patroclus?"

"Zeus," Hera replied, "what will the gods think if you interfere in the name of your son? Many gods have sons fighting in the battle. You cannot show favor to your own family."

Patroclus and Sarpedon fought on viciously. Finally, Patroclus hit Sarpedon, who did not go down quietly. Sarpedon continued to rage and shout orders to Glaucus, one of his men. "Do not lose faith! And do not let them strip my body of armor." Then he closed his eyes and spoke no more.

Glaucus was grief-stricken. He rushed to the slain body of Sarpedon. He tried to protect his friend and prevent his armor from being stripped from his body, but Patroclus was too quick. The Achaean began tossing weapons and bronze to his comrades.

Zeus stepped in to retrieve his son's body. He struck fear in all the men so that they would move away from Sarpedon. Then Zeus carried his favorite son's body up to the heavens to reside in the great hall.

The Achaean generals believed Achilles was back on the battlefield with them. Now they were unshakable. They pushed the Trojan troops back from the shore with great strength and determination. Slowly but surely, the battle moved closer to Troy. However, every time the Achaeans pushed their enemy closer to the city gates, Apollo pushed them back.

"Patroclus," Apollo called, allowing only Patroclus to hear him. "Get back! The proud Trojan city will not fall at your spear. This city will not be destroyed even by Achilles, a far greater warrior than you!"

Hector and his troops arrived at the battle-field. They paused. Hector needed a moment to catch his breath. There was so much confusion. Apollo then appeared at his side.

"Get back into the fight!" he said to Hector. "Return to your city. Rally your soldiers to the gates. Many of the Achaean soldiers are trying to break into your city. Defend it! That man you see there who is trying to drive your troops back to Troy—he is not Achilles. He is Patroclus disguised in Achilles's armor. Face Patroclus and fight him!"

Hector drove his troops back to the gates of Troy to face the Achaean troops. But he did not stop to confront or fight with any other man. He made his way straight to Patroclus.

Patroclus was raging across the battlefield toward the gates of Troy. He killed men quickly and easily. But he did not see death when it was coming for him.

Suddenly, Patroclus felt his helmet being knocked off his head. It tumbled onto the ground and rolled under a chariot. Apollo was taking Achilles's armor off Patroclus's body. The god was helping Hector defeat Patroclus. Then Apollo snapped Patroclus's spear in two. He pulled the breastplate off Patroclus's armor. Patroclus was suddenly exposed and vulnerable. His armor—Achilles's armor—was meant to protect the child of a god. Now Patroclus was just a man left to die on a battlefield.

At that moment, Hector's spear hit Patroclus in the back between the shoulder blades.

Patroclus staggered and tried to pull out the spear. Hector came at him swiftly and hit him with another spear. This time the spear went through Patroclus's chest. The Achaean soldier—Achilles's closest friend—fell to the ground.

Hector growled at him. "You thought you could ruin Troy!" he said. "You thought you could free Helen and her riches. But you will never return to your ship or your homeland. You will die here with nothing. You are nothing!"

"Hector, this may be your victory," Patroclus gasped. "But Zeus and Apollo brought me down, not you. I could have faced twenty Hectors and defeated them all. Your end will soon be here. You will die at the hands of Achilles!" Then Patroclus closed his eyes for the last time.

CHAPTER 15

Achilles Learns the Truth

Menelaus was fighting a few feet from Patroclus and saw him fall. Menelaus let out a terrible cry. He pushed his way through the Trojan army, swinging his sword at every man he saw. He tried to get to Patroclus's body, but there were too many men in the way.

But Ajax and Menelaus arrived just in time to shield their friend's body and protect the armor. They vowed not to let any Trojan near.

Hector made an announcement to his men. "Whoever drags Patroclus's body back to Troy will receive the greatest glory. He will have the fame and fortune of a god," he called out.

This quickly became an intense competition among the Trojans. Men darted in, trying to steal Patroclus's body and armor from Ajax and Menelaus. The Achaeans fought hard to keep Patroclus with them. Somehow, during the confusion of battle, Hector was able to steal the armor.

As Hector ran away with the armor, Ajax called out to him: "Hector, prince of the Trojans! Do you understand that you and your army will soon be overpowered? It is only a matter of time before Achilles learns of Patroclus's death. Then Achilles will return, and you will pay!"

Then Ajax prayed to Zeus.

"Zeus," he called. "We must find Nestor's son to send word to Achilles. He will bring the news swiftly. Please help us find him." Zeus pushed the sun through the clouds. It lit up the battlefield.

Menelaus spotted Nestor's son not far off. He called out to him. "Run to Achilles! Tell him the news of Patroclus. Tell Achilles that Hector is now wearing his armor."

Achilles was on his ship. He was sheltered and safe. But it had been too long since he had heard from Patroclus. Achilles started to worry about his friend.

"I told him to fight one battle, move the Trojans from the ships, then come back. But he has been gone too long . . . "

At that moment, Nestor's son arrived with tears in his eyes. "Achilles, my lord. Our beloved Patroclus has died. The Trojans are right now fighting over his body. And Hector now wears your armor!"

Achilles stared in disbelief. "No," he said softly. "I do not understand your words. Patroclus cannot be dead. Hector cannot be wearing my armor. This is not possible."

Nestor's son did not say another word. He only wept and shook his head sadly. Achilles suddenly realized the truth. His most beloved friend was dead.

The proud warrior was overcome with grief. He leaned against a post and bowed his head. At first, he moaned quietly. As he lifted his head, his cries grew louder until he was screaming. His screams were so loud that they shook the very timbers of his ship. Achilles thrashed and wailed. He fell to the deck. Then he let out a terrible wrenching cry, so loud that all the gods on Mount Olympus heard him.

Achilles's mother, Thetis, also heard her son's terrible cry. She was sitting beside her father, Poseidon, down in the sea. She reached his side in moments. "My darling boy, why do you cry? What hurts you? Zeus has given you everything you want. The Achaeans are suffering terrible losses, all for you. All to show Agamemnon that he should never have disgraced you. What makes you cry?"

"My heart is broken," he said. "My dearest friend is dead. Hector has killed Patroclus and stripped the armor off his body. I have lost the will to live. Only ending Hector's life will bring peace to my darkened heart."

"My son," Thetis said through her own tears. "You know the prophecy. It has been said that you will die a short time after Hector. Asking for Hector's death only means that yours is closer. The fates have ordered this."

"Then let me die now!" Achilles cried. "I let Patroclus go to this death. I did not defend him. I did not fight beside him. I stayed here—protected—on my ship. I let countless men die in battle. Enough is enough! I will put my anger aside. I will return to battle, and I will face the enemy who put an end to Patroclus's life. As for my death, I will meet it whenever it arrives."

"I will not stop you, my son. But you have no armor," Thetis warned. "Hector wears your armor now. Do not leave until I return. I will come back first thing in the morning with armor built by Hephaestus, god of fire!"

Meanwhile, the battle over the body of Patroclus continued. The Achaeans realized they had little chance to drag it to safety. The Trojans kept swooping in to try to steal the body. But the Achaeans were able to fight them off for the time being.

Back at Achilles's ship, Iris the messenger arrived. She was sent by Hera. "Achilles, you must leave now. You must head back to battle and defend your brothers. It is urgent!"

"But I have no armor," he said. "My mother told me to wait. She will bring newly created armor to me in the morning."

"Do not worry," Iris said. "There is a plan. Go to the battlefield and show yourself to the

Trojans. Just make an appearance. Your enemies will be shocked and frightened by the sight of you. That may stop their attacks."

Achilles did as he was told and stood up. Athena appeared beside him and strapped her shield across his back. She crowned his head with a bright light and lit a fire to blaze across the field.

Achilles returned to shore and took his stand by the crumbled wall. He observed all the action. When he had seen enough, he let out a mighty cry that carried all his pain. The Trojans stopped in their tracks.

The Trojans were terrified by the sight of Achilles. He stood, bathed in bright light, at the edge of the battleground. As predicted, the Trojans ran back toward their camp in fear. The Achaeans were finally able to bring Patroclus's body back to safety at their own camp. Achilles returned to camp with them.

That night the Trojans had a long discussion. They had to figure out what to do now that Achilles had returned.

In the Achaean camp, Achilles stood before the generals and soldiers he once had abandoned. "We are broken," he said. "We have all lost dear friends in this long war. We will never have the victory we want. We have lost Patroclus, and I know no greater pain."

The men watched Achilles in silence. Everyone wondered what he would say next.

"But the Trojans will feel a far greater pain," he said. "Although we have lost many noble and loyal men, including Patroclus, the Trojans will lose everything. We will fight this battle, and we will win. I will bury my friend only after I have killed Hector and regained my armor."

The Achaean army gave Achilles a cheer. They were relieved the great warrior had returned. Victory did seem possible once more.

CHAPTER 16

A New Day, a New Battle

Dawn appeared. Thetis arrived with new armor for Achilles. The goddess found her son weeping over Patroclus's body.

She took his hand. "My child, you must leave your friend now. Leave him even though it breaks your heart. I bring you a gift from the god of fire. It is new armor. This armor is finer than any armor a mortal has ever worn!"

"You are right, Mother," he said. "This armor is magnificent. There is nothing finer. I am ready to wear it and go into battle."

Achilles put on his armor and joined the Achaeans on the battlefield. He was greeted with cheers and slaps on the back. He raised his arm to silence the crowd.

"Fellow Achaeans," Achilles shouted. "I am here to fight with each of you to defeat Hector. I am here to avenge the death of Patroclus—not to support King Agamemnon."

Agamemnon addressed Achilles: "I am glad you have returned to us, old friend. I mean to set things right between us."

"But now we must move," said Achilles. "There is no time for talking. We are here to fight, and we are here to win. Let's get to it!"

While Achilles and the Achaeans prepared for battle, Zeus called all the gods for a meeting. Even Poseidon made his way from the sea and joined them in the great hall.

Poseidon was suspicious of Zeus's plans. "Why do you call us all to Mount Olympus? Could this be about the Trojan and Achaean armies facing each other again? Are you concerned that they will burst into flames with anger and violence?"

"You know my plans, Poseidon. You know that I am concerned for these mortals," Zeus said. "I will remain on Mount Olympus to watch the battle from my throne. The rest of you, go down to Earth. Join the Trojans or the Achaeans as you will. You can each decide which side you will support. Achilles fights for the Achaeans. The Trojans now do not stand a chance Achilles is even more powerful after Patroclus's death. We must even the playing field."

The gods went down to earth. Hera, Athena, and Poseidon joined the Achaeans. Hermes, the god of luck, and Hephaestus, the god of fire, followed them. Aphrodite, Ares, and Artemis joined the Trojans.

Zeus filled the skies with lightning and thunder. Poseidon shook the boundless earth and towering mountains. The whole world quaked so violently that Hades, lord of the dead, jumped from his throne and shouted. He feared the world would burst open.

God fought against god, and man fought against man. Achilles searched for Prince Hector on the battlefield. He was full of fury. Any Trojan soldier standing in his way did not have a chance. Achilles cut them down as he searched for Hector. The Achaean warrior was brutal. Even the gods did not want to face Achilles on the battlefield.

Yet someone had to stop him. Apollo went to Aeneas, son of Aphrodite, and spoke in his ear. He persuaded Aeneas to face Achilles.

Aeneas left his ranks. He approached Achilles with long menacing strides. He kept his shield out to protect himself. But Achilles moved quickly. He was like a cat hunting in the wild. He leaped out to capture his prey.

"Aeneas," Achilles said. "Why are you so far from your troops? Are you really so brave? Has Priam promised you treasure if you beat me?"

Aeneas said, "You cannot frighten me with words. I can throw insults, too. And I can throw other things." And with that he flung a spear at Achilles. It clanged against Achilles's massive gold shield.

Achilles sent his own spear flying. Aeneas crouched low and raised his shield high. The spear stuck in the ground behind Aeneas.

Aeneas stood up. He was frightened but brave. Achilles charged at him again. The Achaean was wild, rushing toward his opponent. Achilles lifted a giant boulder over his head. This was a tremendous feat. It weighed a ton, but Achilles raised it with ease. He moved to thrust the boulder at Aeneas. But Aphrodite interfered.

Aphrodite was upset that Apollo had tricked Aeneas into facing Achilles. Aeneas never stood a chance in that battle. Aphrodite had to do something to help. She covered Achilles in mist so thick that he could not see in front of him.

When the fog cleared, Aeneas was gone.

Achilles returned to his troops. He encouraged them to fight harder against the Trojans. "We must all fight strongly. Do not hang back. Join me in fighting with full force!"

Hector was doing the same with his Trojan troops. He encouraged them to put all their power into fighting the Achaeans. Hector kept a close eye on Achilles, always knowing where that warrior was on the battlefield.

Hector, seeing Achilles strike with his sword, heard a familiar cry. The Achaean had stabbed one of his brothers and left him near death.

Hector could bear no more of this. The Achaeans, especially Achilles, had done too much damage. Hector could not stand to lose one more man, especially his brother. Shaking his spear, Hector charged at Achilles. But Achilles spotted Hector coming his way.

Achilles shouted at him, "Come quickly! The sooner you reach me, the sooner you die!"

Hector stood strong. "Achilles, I know you are braver and stronger than I am," he said. "But you have not won yet. I still have my mighty weapon. And perhaps the gods are on my side."

Suddenly, Apollo threw a swirling mist around Hector. Achilles charged at Hector three times. He kept wildly missing his mark. On his fourth attempt, Achilles charged with all his strength. His battle cry was so tremendous that Apollo feared for Hector's life. The god pulled the prince from the battlefield at once. The mist lifted. Achilles realized that Hector was gone. He vowed to put an end to Hector once and for all.

The Achaeans had pushed the Trojan forces away from their ships and back toward Troy. Achilles led the troops, carving a path through the Trojan men with his sword. He killed many and spared none who were in his way.

In the city of Troy, King Priam was watching the battle from his lookout. He saw Achilles driving the Trojan army toward the city walls. Priam now understood that all hope was gone. Achilles's power was too great.

Apollo swooped down from the sky. He landed just outside the city walls as the Trojans approached. Achilles soon arrived, too. Apollo faced Achilles and began to battle him— immortal versus man. During this fight, the Trojans had just enough time to escape.

King Priam opened the gates of Troy to let the Trojan soldiers back in. He watched as the soldiers shot their last spears and arrows at Achilles. The weapons hit his godly armor but did not strike the man.

CHAPTER 17

Achilles and Hector Meet

❧

The men of Troy moved through the gates and into their city. Once the gates closed, they were safe again. The men wiped away their sweat. They quenched their thirst with cool water. They thanked the gods that they had made it home. Only Hector stayed outside the gates. He was waiting for Achilles. Achilles raced toward Troy, shouting for Hector.

King Priam watched from his lookout as Achilles approached the gates. Priam called down to Hector, who was waiting for his enemy:

"Do not stand there, my son! Come inside the gates of the city. Don't you feel Achilles's rage? Don't you see his hatred? I have lost too many sons to this man and this war. Do not fight him here and now!"

Priam cried and tore at his hair. Hector's mother cried and wailed, too. Hector's wife watched silently with tears in her eyes. But Hector stood in front of the gates of Troy.

If he turned back now, he would be considered a coward by his fellow Trojans. He would not be able to hold his head high ever again. Hector could not live in disgrace. To him, that was worse than death.

Hector saw Achilles approach. He saw the rage in Achilles's eyes and was scared. Rather than battle Achilles face to face, Hector ran away in fear. Achilles chased him faster than a wild mountain hawk chases its prey.

They raced around the walls of the city.

Hector ran for his life. Achilles followed. They raced around the city's walls four times.

As the two men reached the fountain for the fourth time, Zeus took out his scales. This war had gone on far too long. The mortals had been fighting for almost ten years. Now gods and goddesses were fighting one another.

Zeus set up the scales and measured the fates of Achilles and Hector. The scales of fate weighed down on Hector's side. Athena flew down to Achilles and gave him the news.

"It is time for you to meet Hector face to face. He is destined to die in this battle. You must seal his fate," she said.

Hector realized he could not run any longer. He turned to face Achilles. "I will run no more, Achilles. Let us end this. But first I will make a pledge to you: if I win this battle, I will return your body to your people. Pledge that you will do the same."

Achilles laughed. "We will have no pledge, Hector! A wolf does not make a pact with his prey. There is no love between us. Draw your spear and let us finish this battle once and for all." Achilles quickly threw his spear. Hector ducked out of the way.

"Ha! You have missed me," Hector mocked Achilles. He pitched his own spear. It hit Achilles's shield dead in the center. A clang rang out, and his spear shattered. Hector was shocked. He did not have another spear. He knew instantly that his fate was to die.

Achilles and Hector drew their swords. They clashed. They lunged. They slashed through the air. At last, Achilles knocked Hector down with his sword.

"You killed Patroclus and stole the armor he was wearing—*my* armor! You thought you would be protected by the gods. But you were wrong. And now you will die," Achilles roared.

Hector begged Achilles to promise that his body would go to his family for a proper burial. Achilles refused.

"I can see that you will have no mercy on me. Your chest is filled with iron, not a heart—" But Hector's speech was cut short by death.

Achilles took back his sword from Hector's body. He then stole Hector's armor. Achilles announced to his soldiers, "Hector is now dead. We need not fear him or his army any longer! And I have killed the man who killed Patroclus. My friend will always live in my heart. I have gotten my revenge for his death."

Achilles's men brought him his chariot. He stood atop it and faced the walls of Troy with great pride. "Your prince is dead!" he shouted. "I have his armor and his body. You are left with nothing!" Achilles then dragged the body of Hector back to the Achaean camp.

CHAPTER 18

The Funeral Games

To celebrate his victory over Hector— and to pay respect to the life of his friend—Achilles hosted funeral games in honor of Patroclus. The Achaean men competed in various sports and challenges. Achilles looked on. But none of this cheered Achilles. He was still drowned in sorrow for his friend. And he still kept Hector's corpse.

Once the games were over, it was time to bury Patroclus. Achilles seemed to grieve even harder for his lost friend. He missed his friendship, his advice, and his humor. One night soon after Patroclus's funeral, Achilles could not sleep. He got up and went to his friend's grave. Achilles dragged Hector's corpse around Patroclus's grave three times. But that did not cure his sadness.

The whole time, Apollo protected Hector's corpse. The god put an invisible shield around the dead warrior. This way his body could not be damaged as it was dragged. Apollo hoped that Hector's family could still bury him with dignity.

Apollo appealed to the other gods. "Many of you stood by the murderous Achilles as he destroyed Hector. At least allow Hector to have a burial that is fitting for a prince. His family needs to see him. He fought well for Troy. His people need to mourn him properly."

Zeus agreed. He declared that Hector's body should be returned to his father. But they could not steal his body back from Achilles. Thetis was always standing guard.

Zeus called Thetis to Mount Olympus. "We

must give Hector's body back to his people. I promise you that we will still give Achilles his rightful glory. But Hector's people need to say good-bye to him. Do what you must to persuade Achilles to give up Hector's body."

Thetis went to her son. She found Achilles wailing at Patroclus's grave. She gently put her hand on her son's shoulder.

"My dear boy," she said. "It is time to bury the bodies. Zeus himself commands you to give Hector's body back to his father."

"I want the Trojans to suffer as I suffer," Achilles cried.

"They do suffer," she said. "They lost many men, including their prince. They lost many battles. Now you must obey Zeus's orders."

"Of course," he sighed. "But they must pay for our losses, too. Whoever brings us payment—treasure and gold—may take the body," Achilles told his mother.

Zeus sent a messenger to tell the news to King Priam. The king sat alone in his bedroom. The wails of the Trojan men and women could be heard throughout the city.

"Achilles will give back your son's body in exchange for treasure," the messenger said. "Send your ransom over to the Achaean ships and retrieve your son. But you must go on your own. Zeus will protect you on your journey."

Priam wasted no time. A wagon full of treasure was prepared. He was an old man, and this was a dangerous mission. But Priam trusted that Zeus would protect him and his driver.

Queen Hecuba said, "Are you a fool, dear husband? You cannot go yourself! How can you trust Achilles? It is too dangerous."

"I must go," Priam said to his wife. "Even if I die at the hands of Achilles, I must get my son's body back. Don't you feel we deserve to say good-bye?" Priam continued his preparation. The king disguised himself as a peasant. Then he climbed into the wagon full of treasure for Achilles.

Queen Hecuba rushed up to the wagon and said, "Quick! Offer wine to Zeus before you leave. Make him happy so he will protect you." King Priam grabbed a jug from his wagon nearby. He poured some wine to the earth and gave generous praise to Zeus.

Zeus looked favorably upon the offering. He sent an eagle soaring over their heads.

"Zeus seems pleased!" Priam told his wife "I will go to the Achaean camp without fear."

Priam arrived at Achilles's tent in the dark of night. He entered the tent and knelt down beside Achilles. He kissed Achilles's hand—the hand that killed so many of his sons.

"I have lost many sons in this war," King Priam said. "Troy has lost too many good men. It will take a long time to recover. But no pain is as great as losing Hector. Pity me, Achilles. I am a broken old man. Let me bury my son with the honor he deserves."

Eventually, Achilles found the strength to speak. "You are a brave man to come here. I could easily kill you now. But I will not hurt you. And I will give you back your son. The gods played with our lives. We were only toys in their games. And now we must suffer. But our sorrow will not bring our loved ones back."

Achilles left the tent. He asked some of his men to prepare Hector's body by carefully wrapping it in robes.

Achilles lifted Hector's body and placed him in Priam's wagon. He felt calm for the first time since Patroclus had died. His thoughts were with his dear friend.

"How long will it take you to honor and bury Hector?" he asked King Priam.

"It will take us nine days to mourn," Priam said. "We will bury him on the tenth day and feast the day after. We will be ready to fight again on the twelfth day."

"Fine," Achilles said. "I give you my word that you will have that time. We will not fight again until Hector is given his full honor."

Priam left the Achaean camp and returned to Troy with his son's body. The entire city mourned and celebrated Hector's life. Helen, in particular, was overcome with grief.

She wept beside his body. "You were always kind to me, my dear brother-in law," she said. "You will be missed for so many reasons."

On the tenth day, Hector's body was buried. On the eleventh day, the entire city of Troy feasted. They shared their sorrow and celebrated the prince's life. On the twelfth day, as King Priam had told Achilles, the Trojan soldiers prepared to meet their enemy again.

What Do *You* Think?
Questions for Discussion
෴

Have you ever been around a toddler who keeps asking the question "Why?" Does your teacher call on you in class with questions from your homework? Do your parents ask you about your day at the dinner table? We are always surrounded by questions that need a specific response. But is it possible to have a question with no right answer?

The following questions are about the book you just read. But this is not a quiz! They are designed to help you look at the people, places, and events from different angles. These questions do not have specific answers. Instead, they might make you think of these stories in a completely new way.

Think carefully about each question and enjoy discovering more about these classic myths.

1. In *The Iliad*, Achilles is the most feared of the Aechaean soldiers. He is widely honored and respected. Do you consider Achilles to be a hero? Are there times in this story when he does not act as a hero?

2. *The Iliad* is a story about the Trojan War. But it is also a story of a quarrel between two mighty warriors: Achilles and Agamemnon. When you read the story, did you side with one or the other? Why? How does their fight affect the larger war?

3. A feud over beautiful Helen is what started the Trojan War. Do you think she is in the

middle of this war? How would you feel if you were Helen? Would you take sides? Which side would you take: Trojan or Achaean?

4. The gods of Mount Olympus seem to take sides in the Trojan War and claim certain humans as their favorites. How do some of the gods choose their sides? How does their involvement change the outcome of certain battles? Do you think the gods should be involved in the Trojan war or in human life at all?

5. Some Achaean and Trojan soldiers know they are favored by certain gods. Does this knowledge affect their behavior in battle? If you knew a powerful figure was always on your side, would it change the way you live your life?

6. Some of the Achaean and Trojan soldiers dare to challenge the gods. Do you think doing so is wise? Can you remember a time when you challenged someone with more power than you? What were the results?

7. Hector and Paris are brothers, both of them sons of King Priam of Troy. In what ways are these two princes different? Are they at all similar? Do you think either of them fits the description of prince?

8. How does the death of Patroclus affect Achilles's decisions? What was he like before his friend's death? What was he like after?

9. Hector and Achilles are both told their fates by the gods. Does this affect their actions during the war?

10. *The Iliad* ends very much the way it began: with the war still going strong. Do you think any progress is made between the Trojans and the Achaeans during this story? What do you think happens after this story ends?

A Note to Parents and Educators

By Arthur Pober, EdD

❧

First impressions are important.

Whether we are meeting new people, going to new places, or picking up a book unknown to us, first impressions can count for a lot. They can lead to warm, lasting memories or can make us shy away from future encounters.

Can you recall your own first impressions and earliest memories of reading the classics?

Do you remember wading through pages and pages of text to prepare for an exam? Or were you the child who hid under the blanket to read with a flashlight, joining forces with Robin Hood to save Maid Marian? Do you remember only how long it took you to read a lengthy novel such as *Little Women*? Or did you become best friends with the March sisters?

Even for a gifted young reader, getting through long chapters with dense language can easily become overwhelming and can obscure the richness of the story and its characters. Reading an abridged, newly crafted version of a classic novel can be the gentle introduction a child needs to explore the characters and story line without the frustrations of difficult vocabulary and complex themes.

Reading an abridged version of a classic novel gives the young reader a sense of independence and the satisfaction of finishing a "grown-up" book. And when a child is engaged with and inspired by a classic story, the tone is set for further exploration of the story's themes, characters, history, and details. As a child's reading skills advance, the desire to tackle the original, unabridged version of the story will naturally emerge.

If made accessible to young readers, these stories can become invaluable tools for understanding themselves in the context of their families and social environments. This is why the Classic Starts series includes questions that stimulate discussion regarding the impact and social relevance of the characters and stories today. These questions can foster lively conversations between children and their parents or teachers. When we look at the issues, values, and standards of past times in terms of how we live now, we can appreciate literature's classic tales in a very personal and engaging way.

Share your love of reading the classics with a young child, and introduce an imaginary world real enough to last a lifetime.

Dr. Arthur Pober, EdD

Dr. Arthur Pober has spent more than twenty years in the fields of early childhood and gifted education. He is the former principal of one of the world's oldest laboratory schools for gifted youngsters, Hunter College Elementary School, and former director of Magnet Schools for the Gifted and Talented for more than twenty-five thousand youngsters in New York City.

Dr. Pober is a recognized authority in the areas of media and child protection and is currently the US representative to the European Institute for the Media and European Advertising Standards Alliance.

Explore These Wonderful Stories in our
Classic Starts™ Library.

Great Expectations

Greek Myths

Grimm's Fairy Tales

Gulliver's Travels

Heidi

The Hunchback of Notre-Dame

The Iliad

Journey to the Center of the Earth

The Jungle Book

The Last of the Mohicans

Little Lord Fauntleroy

Little Men

A Little Princess

Little Women

The Man in the Iron Mask

Moby-Dick

Oliver Twist

Peter Pan

The Phantom of the Opera